*For Benjamin Pollard
to read to his grandparents John and Laura.
We wish you lots of laughter
and resilience, little one.*

First edition 2018. Library of Congress Catalog Card Number pending. ISBN 978-0-7636-9270-4. This book was typeset in Barbedor. The illustrations were done in gouache. Candlewick Press, 99 Dover Street, Somerville, Massachusetts 02144. visit us at www.candlewick.com
Printed in Shenzhen, Guangdong, China. 18 19 20 21 22 23 CCP 10 9 8 7 6 5 4 3 2 1

Angel in Beijing

Belle Yang

CANDLEWICK PRESS

On New Year's Eve, firecrackers scare a white cat into our courtyard and up the ginkgo tree.

I tease her with a pink feather duster.
She skitters down and pounces.

That night she snuggles in bed with me.
"What shall we name her?" Mama asks.
"Let's wait till we get to know her better," I say,
but we end up just calling her Kitty.

Kitty loves to come with me when I bicycle around Beijing.
I clip my new bell onto the handlebar. *Trrring-trrring.*
Niaow-niaow, answers Kitty.

In Beihai Park, a man
is taking a walk with his
huamei birds.
Old people play chess.

Musicians draw their bows across the two strings of their *erhus*.
A barber gives a haircut. When I'm hungry, I stop to buy candied haw fruits on a stick, which I share with Kitty.

On the day of the Dragon Boat Festival,
I take Kitty to Tiananmen Square to see the kites.
It is so crowded, I ring my bell: *Trrring-trrring.*
    Niaow-niaow, says Kitty.
    A Monkey King kite, a butterfly kite,
and a swallow kite fly over our heads.
    Kitty likes the enormous dragon
kite best. Lots of help is needed
to send it up into the sky.

Feathers twirl on its long tail. Kitty jumps out
of my basket and chases after it.

Kitty pounces and catches the dragon's beard.
The kite is lifted into the air. Kitty goes with it!
I hop on my bicycle and race after her.
Trrring-trrring!

Niaow-niaow!

The kite disappears above cypress trees.
By the time I see it again, Kitty is gone.

I ride all over the neighborhood.
Trrring-trrring!
But I hear no reply.

My heart is down in my shoes.

The stars flicker in the sky and crickets chirp, but still Kitty has not come home. I cannot sleep. Maybe she has already forgotten me.

At dawn, when Baba's *huamei* sings in its cage, I bicycle to the Forbidden City. I lock my bike and take off the bell.

I climb Jingshan. Oh, what a big view when the sky is clear!
Trrring-trrring.
But Kitty is not there.

Back on my bike, I ride along the west side of Beihai Park.
Kitty likes to spend hours looking at the rowboats.
Trrring-trrring.
There's no reply.

I go south to Tiantan, the Temple of Heaven.
Maybe she's counting mice under the eaves.
Trrring-trrring.

I visit Liulichang Street. Kitty has good taste in antiques. She likes to watch artists painting, too. *Trrring-trrring.*

I have been searching for a long time.
It's time to go home. I am tired and grumpy.

I take a shortcut through a *hutong* that smells of yummy steamed *baozi*.

Suddenly, a man with a cart steps into my path.

I ring my bell in warning. *Trrring-trrring! Trrring-trrring!*

And guess what? I hear
Niaow-niaow. It's coming from
the other side of a gate.
Trrring-trrring, I ring again.
Niaow-niaow!
I am so excited, I push open
the gate.

There is a granny sitting on a stool,
picking stones out of mung beans.
A white cat is lying across her feet.
Kitty sits up and purrs.

"Where did you get her, Granny?" I ask.

The old lady's face wrinkles into a smile. "She dropped right out of heaven into my lap," she replies, "so I named her Angel. I had been lonely living here by myself."

I do not tell the smiling woman that Kitty once snuggled in bed with me.
I do tell her that I will come to visit both of them as often as I can.